Best
My ~~Worst~~ Sleepover Party

Best
My ~~Worst~~
Sleepover Party

by Anna Morgan and
Dr. Rachael Turkienicz

Second Story Press

Library and Archives Canada Cataloguing in Publication

Morgan, Anna, 1957-
Turkienicz, Rachael, 1959-
My worst/best sleepover party / by Anna Morgan and Rachael
Turkienicz ; illustrated by Heather Castles.

ISBN 1-897187-20-3
ISBN 978-1-897187-20-3

I. Turkienicz, Rachael II. Castles, Heather III. Title.

PS8626.O743M98 2007   jC813'.6   C2007-900561-6

Edited by: Anne Millyard
Designed by: Melissa Kaita

Printed and bound in Canada

*Second Story Press gratefully acknowledges the support of the Ontario Arts
Council and the Canada Council for the Arts for our publishing program. We
acknowledge the financial support of the Government of Canada through the
Book Publishing Industry Development Program.*

 Canada Council   Conseil des Arts
for the Arts   du Canada

ONTARIO ARTS COUNCIL
CONSEIL DES ARTS DE L'ONTARIO

Published by
SECOND STORY PRESS
20 Maud Street, Suite 401
Toronto, ON M5V 2M5
www.secondstorypress.ca

Contents

To our families, Jennie, Jacob, Orly and Ed and to Margalit, Rebecca, Isaac, Ezra, Chava and Vadim. You are our greatest strength and our greatest inspiration.

And we would like to thank those people who helped with their support, their feedback, and insights. The staff at Second Story Press has given us of their time and experience and it is greatly appreciated. We are indebted to Margie Wolfe, Denise Grant, Carolyn Jackson, and Melissa Kaita in particular. Anne Millyard, our editor, brought insights and challenging questions to us each time she read this work. Geraldine Sherman reviewed, commented, and spoke of the characters in this book as if they were real, which lifted our spirits. Early in the process, Dr. Sue Power gave of her time to read this work. Uliana Shimla avidly read each chapter after it was written and shared with us her emotions and memories.

THANKS EVERYBODY!

1

My Best-Made Plans

I did exactly what Mrs. Sharpe said. I asked her if she thought I should have a sleepover party for my birthday this year. She said it was a good idea, but I should ask my parents. I went home from school and asked my mom. Here's what my mom said. She said, "Why, Rose Jessica Singleton, I think that's a great idea." If only she had not allowed it. If only my mom had said it would be too much trouble. If only my mom had told me it would end up so badly, then I would never have done it.

How could both my mom and my teacher be so wrong?

You see, everything was going fine with the planning of the party, that wasn't the problem. We were going to wait to have the party on a Saturday night. It wasn't going to be exactly on my birthday, because this year my birthday was on a Tuesday. But there was enough time between now and then to plan the party and give out the invitations and get all the answers of who was coming and who wasn't coming. I liked the idea of having the party on a Saturday night, even though it wasn't exactly my birthday. Everyone has parties on the weekend and it's okay as long as it's to celebrate the birthday, then the exact day doesn't matter.

"Why don't we have everyone build a pizza at your sleepover party?" asked my mom.

"How would we do that?" I asked.

"Well, we'll have enough pizza dough for each person to stretch and make a personal-sized pizza. Then we would put out all the toppings, like mushrooms and green peppers and olives and stuff like that," she explained.

"Each person can choose her most favorite toppings and put it on her pizza," she said. "That would be lots of fun." I imagined all the funny stuff my friends would do with the toppings. I could already see the green pepper I would hold under my nose and pretend I had a moustache. I could make a face on my pizza with all the toppings. The olives could be the eyes and I could use a big mushroom for the nose and maybe a red pepper for the lips. Maybe we could even have jelly beans and chocolate chips to add for hair and earrings and all kinds of stuff. This was starting to sound like an amazing idea.

"We would make sure everyone had enough pizza sauce to spread on their dough and then they could build their pizzas with the toppings and I would bake them," said mom.

I gave my mom a great big hug. "I love you," I said, "and I love this idea. This is going to be the best party in the history of parties. I can't wait!"

It seemed like a great idea. All the girls in my class would come over and we would all build our pizzas and then we would get into our pajamas and then the real fun would start. Ooooooh, my head was filled with the things we would do. The flashlight games, the scary stories, braiding each other's hair. Maybe my mom would even let us do nail polish with her. Why couldn't it have happened that way? Why couldn't it have worked out as the best party in the history of parties?

The problem wasn't that we couldn't think of things to do or games to play. Mom and me had that all planned out. We bought the pizza dough, we had the sauce and all the crazy toppings we needed. Mom even remembered to buy extra batteries for the flashlight scary stories, and we found all our extra flashlights in case anybody forgot to bring one.

"I know what story I'm going to tell first," I said.

"Which one?" asked mom.

"The one where a whole group of girls goes camping one night by an old cabin and then they hear footsteps in the woods — you know, the one with the escaped crazy guy and the claw — you know."

"That one might be too scary for some of your friends," she said.

"Not *my* friends," I said, "they tell worse stories than that. You should hear the one about the wicked, evil step-mother who would hang mice by their tails over the bathroom sink every morning." I didn't finish telling my mom that story because I don't like that one. Also, I could see mom's eyebrows were going up on the outside and down on the inside. This was never a good sign.

"Well, maybe we won't tell that one," I said.

"I hope not," said mom.

Later that day we bought packages of pony-tail elastics for the braids and looked at bright, bright nail polish colors because mom said yes to doing our nails.

The terrible problem didn't happen when we were planning our activities. The problem started when for no good reason, no reason that made any sense, no reason that I could even understand, Hailey and Bailey told me I couldn't invite Stacey to my party.

"What do you mean I can't invite Stacey?" I asked.

"Well, we just think that if you invite Stacey then maybe we won't come," said Hailey and Bailey.

"But Stacey is my best friend. We always hang around together. And you guys always join us, too. Even yesterday it was all four of us at recess. Didn't we all play together? We made teams, it was me and Stacey on one team and you two on the other team. We had a great time playing together. Did something happen? Did Stacey do something? Did she say something? What did she do? Oh my goodness, I really should know what she did, maybe she needs to say she's sorry and that will

6

solve everything. I already told her about the party and she said she's coming and everything. I really should know what she did 'cause she's my best friend. You really should tell me what she said and I'll get her to say she's sorry." I realized I was maybe talking too much, so I stopped talking.

"We didn't say she did anything," said Hailey.

"We didn't say she said anything," said Bailey.

Hailey and Bailey looked at each other. Bailey stared at me while Hailey said, "We just said that if you invite Stacey then we're not coming."

I Can Fix This, Can't I?

I couldn't believe it. How could I not invite Stacey?
Why are Hailey and Bailey so mad at her? I was with
them the whole time at recess, I didn't see anything
happen. All yesterday Stacey seemed perfectly fine.
She wasn't upset or crying in the bathroom or anything. Everything seemed just as it always does. You
know what? We even had a fantastic special recess
because we had to try on the make-up for the play
that we're planning. I even remember what Stacey
said when Hailey brought all her make-up stuff.

"You won't believe the make-up that Hailey brought to school," said Stacey.

"She always has the best stuff," said Paige. "I wish I had make-up glitter for the eyes like Hailey has."

"Did you see her strawberry lip gloss that can hang around your neck on a string?" asked Melissa.

"You're so lucky," said Natalie when Hailey came over. "Your mother buys you all this stuff for the play. My mother says I have to be older before I can have any make-up."

"My mother didn't buy this for the play," said Hailey. "This stuff is mine. I got it for my birthday and no one is allowed to use it without my permission."

Maybe Stacey used Hailey's make-up without asking her. I bet that's the problem. Think, think, *think*, did she do that? But I thought so much I could feel my brain getting hot. I'm positively certain that Stacey didn't use anything without asking. I was with her the whole time. You know what? Now that I remember it, Stacey didn't get any make-up at all. Hailey wouldn't let her use any of the make-up. You know what? I was having so much fun I didn't even notice that Stacey didn't have any eye glitter or strawberry lip gloss on.

There's no way that Hailey is mad at Stacey for touching her make-up because I'm positively certain she never did.

When we came in from recess, Mrs. Sharpe gave us back our math tests. Stacey smiled and told me she did pretty well on the test.

That's it! That's got to be it. Maybe Hailey and Bailey are mad at Stacey because she's good at math. But why would it bother them if she's good at math? Hailey is good at reading and Bailey is pretty good at spelling and nobody ever cared before, so why would it be bad if Stacey is good at math?

I found Bailey standing in line at the water fountain. I had to find out.

"It's because she's good at math, right?" I asked.

"What?" asked Bailey.

"Math. Stacey's good at math. That's why you're mad at her, right? It's because she's good at math — but you're good at spelling," I explained.

"What are you talking about?" Bailey asked.

"The party, my sleepover, you don't want Stacey there because she's good at math, right?"

"Don't be silly. Why would I care how Stacey does at math?" Bailey asked.

"Then it's not the math test we got back from Mrs. Sharpe?" I asked.

"I don't know what you're talking about. Hang on, it's my turn to take a drink," she said as she bent down to drink the water. "By the way, I'm really looking forward to your party," Bailey shouted over her shoulder as she skipped away from the water fountain.

What was I going to do now? I still remember standing at school this morning and letting all the girls know about my party. At recess, everyone was asking me questions.

"Where are you having your party?" asked Marianne.

"Is it a morning party or an afternoon party?" asked Judy. "My mom said that she's tired of morning parties on the weekend, which is the only time she can get some sleep except she always has to get up to take someone to a morning party. She said she's putting her foot down and there'll be no more morning parties if she can help it. Please don't say it's a morning party. I'll just die if I can't come. You can't make it a morning party."

Before I could answer, Samara butted in.

"Is there going to be chocolate milk at your party? I'm lactose intolerant."

"Yeah, me too," said Melissa.

"I'm allergic to peanuts," said Jessica, "so you can't have any peanuts. I carry an epi-pen but my sister said that if I have to use the pen then it's already too serious for the pen so your parents should call 911 and tell them it's an emergency and I could die."

"I can't have any fish," said Paige. "I'm not really allergic, but it makes me puke and I don't think you want me puking at your party."

Then everyone started guessing what kind of party I was having. Ashley said it should be a pottery party. Natalie said it should be a gymnastics party, that's the best thing. Kaitlin said the best party to have is a fashion show party at the Princess Palace and make sure you tell them to include the runway show even though it's extra. Kim kept saying that she had a trampoline party and nothing is as good as that.

"GUYS!!" I finally shouted. "Here are the invitations. It's a sleepover party. It's going to be great. We're going to play games and tell stories and do our nails and our hair and make pizzas and have flashlights. It's all night so there's no morning driving and tell your moms to call my mom so she can make sure not to have chocolate milk or peanuts or fish or … well, or anything else."

Just then, Bailey flipped her curly, dark hair back in her Bailey-flipping-her-hair-back kinda way and then she shouted at everyone: "Gee, I think I'm going to have to come late to a sleepover party because I go to the movies on Saturday night."

"Wow, really?" asked Paige. "What movie did you see last time?"

"I saw the movie about the guy and the girl who go around in their car and go from town to town. You wouldn't believe the things they did," said Bailey.

"Ooooh, I know about that movie. My brother went to see that with his friends. My dad wouldn't even let him talk about it when I was in the room. You saw that movie? You're kidding!" said Melissa.

"Yeah, it's no big deal. I always go to adult movies. But I'll tell you about it at lunch," said Bailey. "Rose, don't you want to give out your invitations?"

That's when I handed out the invitations. The

first invitation had Stacey's name on it because Stacey is my best friend. Stacey has been my best friend since kindergarten. We liked each other right from the very first day and we've been together in the same class since then.

"This is a great idea," said Stacey.

"I know," I said, "I'm so excited I can't wait. You know what? Maybe you should come over in the morning and help me and my mom get ready for the party."

"Wow, that would be fantastic. I'll ask my mom, but I'm sure she'll say yes," said Stacey.

So now what was I supposed to do? I can't figure out why Hailey and Bailey would say that if Stacey comes they won't come. It's not because she's good at math, I already checked that. So what could it be? Maybe it has something to do with Stacey's family. Let's see, she has three brothers. Hey, maybe it's because she has all those brothers and Hailey and Bailey are afraid that Stacey will tell her brothers about girl stuff from the party.

Maybe that's it. It's because Stacey has brothers, that's why they don't want her there.

But I can't do anything about that. How can I fix it so Stacey doesn't have brothers? That's silly. But maybe I can tell Hailey and Bailey that Stacey would never tell her brothers about our secret party stuff. I know she never would, because I share lots of secrets with Stacey and she's never told anyone, and for sure not her brothers. If she told her brothers then I would know, because I see them whenever I go over there to play and for sure they would tease me if she broke her promise to keep my secrets. I know Stacey can be trusted, so all I have to do is tell Hailey and Bailey that they can trust Stacey. That will for sure fix this.

I waited until after school and I saw Hailey standing in the schoolyard waiting for her carpool. I wasn't sure if I should speak to her because she was practicing the steps and moves from the latest music video and I didn't want to interrupt her. Once, Natalie interrupted her and Hailey wouldn't let anyone speak to Natalie all day. Hailey is very serious about some things, like her dance steps, her make-up and her blonde hair (she blow dries it every morning and always talks about how long it takes) and she keeps reminding us how much she looks like that famous rock star (I never remember her name). I guess she looks okay.

I decided to wait a few minutes until she took a break.

"Hi, Hailey," I said.

"Oh, hi, Rose," she answered. "I'm really looking forward to your party."

"Yeah," I said, "so am I. Can I ask you something?"

"Sure," said Hailey.

"Well, I've been thinking about this whole Stacey not being invited to my party thing that you said this morning," I said.

"Yeah, well I hope you've already told her she's uninvited and she can't come," Hailey said.

"But I don't think I have to do that," I said, "because I figured out how to solve the problem."

"What problem?" asked Hailey.

"The one about Stacey coming to the party. I know it's because of her brothers and you think she's going to tell her brothers all our girl stuff. But really she's not because she's really not like that. I know, because I'm her best friend. Stacey can be trusted to keep our secrets. She never breaks her promise and I know that if we ask her to promise not to tell that she will definitely promise. You know what? I'll ask her to promise right now so you can be super sure and then this whole thing will be fixed," I said. I was ready to find Stacey and get her to not only promise but pinky swear it.

"I'm sorry, Rose," said Hailey, "I don't know what you're talking about. I couldn't care less if Stacey has brothers. I have a brother too, so what? Don't make her promise anything 'cause it won't matter. I don't want to talk about her anymore, just make sure she's not coming to the party."

"But I can't do that," I said, "I already invited her."

"Well tell her you changed your mind," she said, "or if you want she can still come but Bailey and me definitely won't be there."

"Hailey!" shouted her carpool friends. "Come on, we're waiting!"

"Bye," said Hailey, "see you tomorrow."

This was the first day that I gave out my invitations. I was so excited and I had everything all planned and it should have been a fantastic day. I could feel my eyes starting to get tears in them and I got so angry I couldn't stand it. Why did Mrs. Sharpe say this was a good idea? Why did mom give me those invitations? I was so mad, I felt like screaming my head off.

I went home and stared at my plate all through dinner. Afterwards, I went into my room and closed the door. I think mom was wondering what happened, but you know what? Let her wonder, I was just too mad at her to explain and besides, this is all her fault.

❀

3

We Can Fix This, Can't We?

I was so mad when I got to my room that I didn't even get undressed and into my pajamas. I didn't even brush my teeth or brush my hair or choose which book to read or close my blinds or anything I'm supposed to do. I was so mad, I just got under my covers and pulled them up over my head and started to cry.

Who needs Hailey and Bailey anyway? I don't care if they come to my stupid party, they can just stay at home and miss out on the best party in the history of parties. But really, I do care. Hailey and Bailey are always the ones telling everyone what game we're going to play at recess. They're always the ones who make the jokes in class that everybody laughs at. Sometimes they make a joke about someone in the class and that's a little mean, but no one ever tells them to stop, and ever since I can remember everyone has wanted them to come to their parties and to play with them.

Last week at Melissa's party, they brought the best present ever. It was a whole kit for doing your nails and your toenails and it had stuff in it I've never even seen before in all my life. It even had a toe ring and everybody said 'ooooh' and 'aaaah' when they saw the toe ring. I wondered if a toe ring would feel really weird inside your sock, but nobody asked that question so I didn't either.

And when it was time for us to watch the scary movie video, Hailey and Bailey were so funny with their shouting things at the movie. When the girl was about to open the door with the zombie behind it, Hailey even shouted, "Watch out! It's Mrs. Sharpe behind the door!" Everybody laughed. I thought it was a little bit mean but also a little bit funny.

At the parties Hailey and Bailey are so much fun and do such crazy great things that I don't know why suddenly they're being so mean to Stacey. I've thought of everything that could be the problem but it doesn't seem to be fixing anything. Just as I was turning all of this in my head, trying to figure out how I can fix this when nothing I tried is working — that's when I heard the door open.

"Rose," said mom, "you have a phone call."

"Who is it?" I asked. Maybe it's Hailey saying she's really coming or maybe it's Bailey to tell me she made a mistake about Stacey.

"It's Stacey," mom answered.

"Oh," I said. "Um, okay, I guess, alright, I'm coming."

I can't believe it. Stacey's the last person

I want to talk to. You know, this would all go away if Stacey wasn't always around me. I don't know why Hailey and Bailey are doing this to me. Things would be so much easier if I just did what they said.

"Hello," I said into the phone.

"Hi," said Stacey. "Whatcha doing?"

"Nothing," I said.

"Oh. Wanna get together?"

"No," I said.

"Oh. Are you busy?" she asked.

"No," I said, "I just don't want to."

Stacey paused for a minute and then said, "Okay. I guess I'll see you tomorrow."

"I guess," I said and hung up the phone.

Could this day get any worse, I asked myself as I walked back to my room, closed the door and got back under my covers. I heard the door open.

"Rose," said mom, "It's Stacey again."

"Tell her I can't come to the phone," I mumbled.

"Why would I tell her that?" mom asked.

"Because I can't talk to her now because if I talk to her then it will only make things worse and because if I don't talk to her, then all this should get better … that's why!" I said.

"Rose, I want you to wait right here, I'll be back in a minute," said mom.

I stayed under my covers feeling terrible about what I did to Stacey, but what else was I supposed to do? I thought if I keep Stacey away from me then I would feel better because then I could tell Hailey and Bailey that I would keep Stacey away from the party. But I don't feel good, I think I feel even worse about what I just did to Stacey.

I DON'T GET THIS!!

"Rose," asked mom, "are you okay?"

"Please go away," I said, trying not to sound like I was crying.

"Rose, honey, can you please tell me what's wrong?" she asked.

I poked my head out from under the blanket and saw my mom standing in my room. I don't think she knew how bad she made my life today at school.

"Rose, are you crying?" asked mom.

"Well I think you'd cry too if you had the terrible day I had," I burst out. "It's been the worst day of my life and it was supposed to be so good. Why did you let me give out my invitations today? I don't know what I'm going to do now. How do I fix this?" I was crying and hugging mom very tight because by now she was already sitting on my bed and holding me.

"Oh my goodness," she said. "What on earth happened at school today?"

"I gave out my invitations and everyone was really happy about the sleepover idea. But then, later, Hailey and Bailey came to me and said that I can't invite Stacey to my party or they won't come."

"I'm sorry," mom said, "say that again."

"You know Hailey and Bailey, the two girls that always hang out together and they're the funniest girls in the class and they always have the best ideas for games and things?"

"I know Hailey and Bailey," mom said. "Go on."

"Well, just like that and I can't figure out why, but they said that if I invite Stacey to my party then they're not coming. I thought it was because she's good at math, but it's not. I thought it was because she has all those brothers, but it's not. I told them I already invited her, but they said it doesn't matter. If they don't come to my party then none of the other girls will come either because they'll tell everyone they're not coming and then everyone will be busy and say they're not coming either. What do I do?!" I was already almost shouting because I was just so mad and the more I was explaining it, the more I just couldn't understand and there was no way to fix all this mess.

Mom was quiet for a minute. She looked right at me, right into my eyes, but she didn't say anything. She hugged me to her chest and she smoothed my hair and I could feel her cheek on my head, but for a long, long time she didn't say anything. It seemed like hours and then I heard her ask me a question.

"Is that why you wouldn't take Stacey's call?"

"Oh Mom, I don't know what to do! I thought that if I'm not friends with Stacey, then I could make this better, so I was mean to her on the phone and didn't even take the phone when she called back. But I don't feel better now, I feel even worse now because I hurt my best friend's feelings. I really don't know what to do anymore."

"Why did you think being mean to Stacey would make you feel better?" asked my mom.

"Because then I would be doing what Hailey and Bailey want. Then they would come to my party. Isn't it easier to just give them what they want? Why do I have to have this great big problem

when I'm just trying to have my party? It's not fair!"
I said.

"You're right, Rose," mom said. "It's not fair.
And you're also right that giving in to Hailey and
Bailey is the easy thing to do. And I think you're
also right in feeling terrible about it, so maybe the
easy thing to do isn't the right thing to do."

I thought about that for a while. It sure would
be easy to just give in, but it won't make me feel
better and I really do like Stacey and I don't think
she's done anything wrong.

"I won't uninvite Stacey to my party," I said.

"I'm glad to hear you say that," mom said. "It
does sound like you had a really terrible day today.
Does Mrs. Sharpe know about what happened?"

"Well, I didn't tell her anything. She always
says that we have to figure out our stuff by ourselves," I explained. "She says that part of growing
up is to not have to come to the grown-up every
time someone says something that bothers us or
does something that upsets us. We're supposed to

tell a grown-up if someone is hurting us or hitting us or doing something dangerous, but not for stuff like this."

"Rose," said mom, "someone could get very hurt by this so I'd like to speak to Mrs. Sharpe and

see what ideas she might have. No wonder you're so upset. What a terrible day. You know, when I have such a terrible day I usually find that sitting in my bed with my clothes on and the blankets over my head doesn't really make me feel much better."

"No, I guess it wasn't really making me feel better," I said, and I could feel the tears starting to come back.

"I have an idea," she said. "Why don't you get into your pajamas and get all washed up and we can sit together in the big comfy chair downstairs and read our books together. I think maybe I could even make some hot chocolate and at least we can end the day with something nice."

Wow, I thought, hot chocolate on a school night. Maybe today can end with something good after all. I guess mom didn't mean to make my day so terrible and maybe when she talks to Mrs. Sharpe, things will get all fixed at school. Maybe this can still be the best party.

"Okay," I said, "you get started on the hot

chocolate and I'll be there in two seconds." I ran out of my room, reached the bathroom, didn't have my pajamas. Ran back to my room, grabbed my pajamas, reached the bathroom, didn't have my brush. Ran back to my room, grabbed my brush, dropped my pajamas, reached the bathroom, couldn't find my pajamas and was too out of breath to run back.

My mom was laughing in the kitchen. "It's not funny," I shouted.

"Yeah," she said, "it really is."

I couldn't help but laugh with her. "Okay," I said, "it really is."

I finally managed to get washed up and in my pajamas and went downstairs with one of my favorite books. I was just getting ready to snuggle in the chair with mom and the hot chocolate, when I heard mom and dad talking in the kitchen.

"You can't be serious," said dad. "You're telling me that two girls are trying to take over Rose's sleepover party?"

"Pretty much," said my mom. "I know how quickly these things can get out of control."

"I don't know," said dad, "I've never been a little girl, but isn't this the sort of thing that girls growing up should take care of by themselves?"

"Well, I was a little girl once and I remember that no matter what anyone would try on their own, most times it just got worse," said mom. "I think I need to speak with the teacher, Mrs. Sharpe, and try to stop this right away."

"Okay, but when would you have time to speak with Mrs. Sharpe? Your whole week is busy with meetings at work," said dad.

"This is definitely more important," mom answered. "We can't leave Rose to handle this on her own. I'll cancel my morning meeting and see Mrs. Sharpe first thing when I drop Rose off at school."

"Do you really think it's that important?" asked dad.

"There's no question," mom said. "Some

things about growing up are best left to themselves, but I think this isn't one of them. I want Rose to come out of this learning the right way to deal with these problems."

Great, I thought, thank goodness, 'cause I really don't know what to do. Though I think right now I should tiptoe down the hall and wait in the snuggle chair ... uh oh ... I have to sneeze. Okay, think of something else ... okay, look at the picture on the wall ... okay, try to — AAAAHCHOOO!!

Dad and mom looked at me for a second before dad said, "*Gezundheit.* So, Rose, how was your day?"

"Not the best," I said, "but tomorrow will be better."

Boy, was I ever wrong about that.

4

I Can't Believe My Ears

The next morning I woke up so excited. Mom was going to school with me and she was going to talk to Mrs. Sharpe and everything was going to get fixed and we could go back to planning for my party.

"What color should the loot bags be?" I asked at breakfast.

Mom smiled when she answered, "I was going to suggest gold because it's one of your favorite colors."

"That's a great idea," I said. Gold loot bags for my golden party with all my golden friends. "We'll have a golden time," I said out loud.

We got to school and I could feel that I was still smiling.

"I'm so excited about your party," said Melissa as we walked through the school yard.

"Yeah, me too," yelled Kirsten.

"I can't wait," shouted Paige.

"My mom loves the sleepover idea," said Judy. "She said more people should think of having sleepover parties so she doesn't have to get up and drive in the morning. She even said that it would be okay to do sleepovers for every party but she wants to know what time she has to get me. Can I stay for lunch or dinner?"

I couldn't really answer anybody because mom kept holding my hand and we walked pretty fast through the school yard to get to Mrs. Sharpe.

"She's probably setting up the room for

the morning," said mom. "I know you need an appointment or the teachers won't talk to you, but this is important enough that I'm sure Mrs. Sharpe will find the time to meet us."

I don't think mom was talking to me when she was saying all this so I didn't bother answering. But I would never tell mom that I think she's talking to herself. I might hurt her feelings.

Mrs. Sharpe was coming out of the Teachers' Lounge holding a cup of coffee. I remembered the hot chocolate from last night and started smiling again.

"Oh, Mrs. Sharpe," said mom, "I'm so glad to catch you before class."

"Oh, good morning Mrs. Singleton. I didn't expect to see you this morning," said Mrs. Sharpe.

"Actually, I was wondering if I could speak with you for a few minutes," mom said.

"To be honest, I was just going to set up the room and get ready for the day. I'd be happy to meet with you if you call the school office and make an appointment," Mrs. Sharpe replied.

Mom dropped her voice into her low, whispering, something-very-serious-to-talk to-you-about tone. "Please, it's rather important."

Mrs. Sharpe looked at her for a minute and then said, "Of course, follow me."

We followed Mrs. Sharpe into the classroom and mom began to tell her everything that happened with the invitations and Stacey and Hailey and Bailey. Mrs. Sharpe turned to me and asked, "Are you sure you understood Hailey and Bailey? Maybe they meant something else."

"Oh, I'm very certain," I said. "Do you think you can help me fix this so we can get back to planning my party?" I asked.

"I think we could probably fix this up pretty fast," said Mrs. Sharpe. "Mrs. Singleton, the latest research is showing that in situations like this it's best to bring all the parties together to deal with the issue head on."

I didn't understand everything Mrs. Sharpe said, but I think she meant that we all had to talk so we could plan all the parties together. I'm not sure I want to plan all my parties with everyone. But maybe that would be the way to solve this. Maybe this is one of Mrs. Sharpe's good ideas.

"Rose," asked mom, "what do you think?"

"I think that's a great idea," I said. I couldn't wait to fix this.

"Please wait here," said Mrs. Sharpe, "I'll call Hailey and Bailey in from the yard and we'll have this cleared up in no time."

While she was gone, I could see that my mom didn't look as happy as I felt.

"Is everything okay?" I asked.

"I'm not so sure this is a good idea," she said.

"Why not?" I asked, but before she could answer, Mrs. Sharpe came back with Hailey and Bailey.

"Girls," said Mrs. Sharpe. "I'm glad we're all here and we can clear up a misunderstanding. Rose and her mom came in this morning to bring to my attention a problem that came up with Rose's party."

"A problem?" asked Hailey.

"What kind of problem?" asked Bailey.

"It seems," said Mrs. Sharpe, "you girls told Rose you wouldn't come to her party if Stacey is invited. Is this true?"

"Of course not," said Hailey.

"Why would we say that?" asked Bailey.

I couldn't believe my ears.

"You told me yesterday that I should tell Stacey not to come. Don't you remember? You told me that if she was invited then you wouldn't come. I asked you if it was the math test and you said no. I asked you if it was the brothers and you said no. I told you I already invited her and you said it didn't matter." I was starting to feel the tears coming back again. "Don't you remember?!"

"Why Rose Singleton," said Bailey, "are you trying to get us into trouble?"

"We never would say that," said Hailey, but she was staring right at me and I knew she knew.

Mrs. Sharpe looked at me and at both the girls and then said, "Girls, did you talk to Rose about her party at all? Did you say anything that maybe was misunderstood?"

"Oh," said Hailey, "I told Rose that I was really excited about her party but that I hope I can go because maybe I would be busy."

"Yes," said Bailey, "I heard her say that and then I said the same thing. I said I hope I can go because maybe I'll be busy that day."

"That's not true!" I shouted.

"Okay," said Mrs. Sharpe, "thank you girls. I'll walk you back to the yard now."

After they left I looked at mom and said, "They didn't say that, Mom, they said … "

"I know," she said. "That's what I was afraid of. I'm just going to speak to Mrs. Sharpe for a few minutes when she gets back."

Soon Mrs. Sharpe came back and went right

to my mom and said, "There's not a whole lot I can do right now. I think the whole thing was probably a misunderstanding. These girls can sometimes be difficult but I've never seen them be outright mean. I'm sure Rose believes they said something about Stacey, but without the girls admitting it, I really can't assume they did."

Mom listened quietly and then looked at me. "Rose," she said, "why don't you forget about this for the rest of today. Maybe being called in to talk to Mrs. Sharpe will make Hailey and Bailey change their minds and the whole thing will just fix itself."

"I hope so," I said.

"Rose," said Mrs. Sharpe, "would you like to stay inside and be my helper until everyone comes in?"

"Oh," I almost shouted, "I'd love that!"

I love staying inside and helping Mrs. Sharpe. She lets me put out the papers on the desks and clean the blackboard erasers by smacking them together outside. I love doing that and pretending to play a tune with the erasers when I bang them together.

"Thank you," said mom to Mrs. Sharpe.

"I'm sure it will all sort itself out," she said. "It always does."

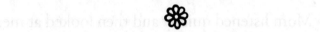

5

My Favorite Games

After my mom left to go home, I was feeling good that Mrs. Sharpe had made me her helper. And maybe mom was right. Maybe Hailey and Bailey were worried now that Mrs. Sharpe knows and my mom knows. Well, they should be plenty worried. I was on my way outside to bang the erasers together when I saw Hailey and Bailey standing and talking at the door that goes outside.

"Excuse me," I said, "I need to get outside to clean these erasers. Mrs. Sharpe asked me to be her helper this morning."

"I can't believe you did that," said Hailey.

"I can't believe you told and tried to get us in trouble," said Bailey.

"My mom wanted to talk to Mrs. Sharpe and clear all this up," I said. "I tried talking to both of you yesterday, but you weren't listening."

"Well we're listening now," said Bailey. "Bet you're pretty happy with things now because you told."

"I still can't believe you told," said Hailey.

"I didn't know what else to do," I said. "All I want is for everyone to have fun at my party. Why is that so hard?"

"Oh yeah," said Hailey, "about your party, well, I wouldn't come now if you paid me."

"Yeah," said Bailey, "me too. You couldn't pay me enough money to come to your party."

"Okay, fine," I said. "Don't come. I don't know what else to do. I tried everything and you know what? This is easier, 'cause now Stacey will never know what you did and her feelings won't be hurt and she can come and we'll just have a fantastic time and you'll miss it. Fine with me."

I walked away and went to clean the erasers. I have to say, I didn't have any fun at all cleaning them. I just hit them together as hard as I could. I smashed them together and I bashed them together and I slam-banged them together until my arms were aching.

When I walked back to the door to go into the classroom I could see that Hailey and Bailey were watching me. They were whispering and looking at me. I just hate that. Just then I saw Stacey running across the schoolyard, waving.

"Rose," shouted Stacey. "Wait up!"

"Hi Stacey," I answered. "Come on, hurry and catch up. Boy, am I glad to see you."

"What's wrong?" asked Stacey, when she finally caught up to me.

"I don't know if I want to talk about it right now, I'm just glad to see you," I said.

"Okay," said Stacey. "Well, let me know if you

want to tell me. By the way, I was thinking about playing a new game, want to hear about it?"

"Sure," I said, even though I wasn't in the mood for a new game, I sure didn't want to have to explain to Stacey everything that's happened the last two days.

"Well, it's kind of like Freeze Tag and kind of like Hide-and-Seek and kind of like Red Rover all mixed together," said Stacey. "First you find a place to hide and then the person who's 'It' comes to find you. When they find you, then you have to freeze until the next person is found and then when two people are frozen then the person who's 'It' calls out 'Bingo' and then everyone who's frozen runs together and holds hands to make a big chain and the person who's 'It' has to run through like Red Rover. Wanna play?"

"Um, sure," I said, even though I wasn't really listening to all of it and wasn't really in the mood for any new game and I couldn't really imagine even playing something new like that. But I could see how excited Stacey was.

"Why don't we play it at recess?" I suggested.

"Great," said Stacey. "I can't wait. Are you feeling any better now?"

"You know what?" I said. "I really am feeling kind of better. Thanks, I think hearing about your new game really did help."

"Glad to be of service," she said. "Hey, do you remember the time Mrs. Sharpe sneezed and couldn't find a tissue and walked around the class with her hand over her nose and I brought her the tissue from my pocket that I only used once and she said, 'No, thank you' and I said, 'Glad to be of service anyway' and she didn't laugh. Do you remember that?"

I started laughing. "Stacey," I said, "sometimes you're so funny."

"I am?" she asked.

"Yeah, sometimes you say such funny things and sometimes you don't even know it."

"Well, thank you, I guess," said Stacey.

"Glad to be of service," I said.

Just then the bell rang and we all lined up to go to the classroom. I didn't see Hailey or Bailey anywhere, which was just fine with me because I didn't want to see them at all anymore. In fact, if I didn't see them for the rest of the day that would be just fine with me too.

"Hi, Melissa," I said.

Melissa didn't answer me.

"Maybe she didn't hear you," said Stacey.

"That's kind of strange," I said, "she walked right beside me."

"Hi, Melissa," I said even louder, but Melissa wouldn't answer me. Just as I was about to go up and ask her if everything was okay, I saw that the school doors opened and our line was going in.

"I wonder what happened to Melissa?" I asked Stacey.

"I don't think anything happened," she said. "I think she just didn't hear you. Are you okay? Why would you think something happened? That's silly. She just didn't hear you."

"I don't know," I said, "it just feels weird."

After we went into the classroom everything was fine. The morning was kind of fun because Mrs. Sharpe had games set up for us. I love math games and spelling games and we had both of them that morning. Stacey and I were in the same group each time and we just laughed and laughed.

That morning we were playing my favorite spelling game. If you were a cow, you could only say words that have two 'o's in them 'cause your first word was 'moo'.

"Moose," I said.

"Loose," said Stacey.

"Choose," I said.

"Caboose," said Stacey.

"Goose," I said.

I was having so much fun with Stacey that I even forgot all about Hailey and Bailey. Who cares anyway? Okay, yesterday was a bad day and this morning was pretty bad too, but at least it's over now and so they won't come to my party, but at least the bad part is over and everything will go back to normal now.

"What's everyone laughing about?" asked Stacey.

We looked around the room and saw the kids walking over to the spelling group next to the window. We had to see what all the fun was so we walked over too.

I saw all the other girls in the class sitting in a circle with Hailey and Bailey leading the spelling game, but with an extra fun part.

"You're out!" shouted Hailey to Kirsten.

"Oh no," said Kirsten, laughing. "I can't believe I missed that one."

"What are they doing?" I whispered to Paige, who was sitting outside the circle watching.

"It's the best game ever, even though I got out first," she said. "Hailey taught us to play. You have to use the same spelling words as before, only now you have to say them to a clapping rhythm. Two taps on your knees and two claps with your hands. But when you tap your knees you have to say the spelling word that rhymes with the word before it. If you miss your rhythm by even one beat then you're out. It goes really fast and it's really smart and really fun."

I walked away and tapped Stacey on the shoulder. We walked back to our desks and kept playing our own spelling game. We tried to play the fun one that Hailey invented but somehow it just wasn't as much fun with only two people. Still, we started laughing again and getting back to having our own fun. I guess things weren't so terrible after all.

That's what I thought until the bell rang and recess started.

6

Worse and Worse

Stacey and I ran outside as soon as the student monitors opened the doors to the schoolyard.

"Let's play my new game," said Stacey.

"Great idea," I said. "How many people do we need to play?"

"Hmm, we need someone to be 'It' and at least two more people so they can make the chain for the Red Rover part. So I guess we need three or more, and you and me are already playing, so we need just one more person to join us so we can start," explained Stacey.

"Okay, how about asking Paige to come and play?" I suggested. "She's walking this way. Quick call her over."

"Paige!" shouted Stacey.

"PAIGE!" shouted Stacey.

"**PAIGE!**" shouted Stacey.

But Paige just walked past us to go play skipping. I looked at Stacey who looked back at me and we both just shrugged our shoulders up and down, which means I didn't know why Paige didn't come over to us and Stacey also didn't know.

"Okay, how about asking Melissa to come and play our game?" I suggested.

"MELISSA!" shouted Stacey.

"OH, MELISSA!" shouted Stacey.

"HEY! **MELISSA!**" shouted Stacey.

But Melissa just walked past us and started talking to Paige.

"Um, I'm not sure why no one is answering. Maybe they can't hear you." I said. "Let me try. Oh look, there's Natalie and she's just sitting down by the swings doing nothing." I took a deep breath in and then I called out, "NATALIE!"

"WHOA! NATALIE!" I yelled.

"NATALIE! NATALIE! **NATALIE!**" I screamed.

But Natalie looked over at us, got up and walked past us. She kept walking until she was standing with Paige and Melissa in a small circle talking together.

"What's going on with everyone?" asked Stacey.

"I'm not sure," I said. And suddenly we noticed that Paige and Melissa and Natalie were all walking over to us.

"We've decided to say something to you," said Melissa.

"Yes, we think you should know something," said Paige.

"Here's why we won't talk to you," said Melissa.

"We don't talk to people who get other people into trouble for no good reason, and then tell on those people and don't even bother to apologize and say they're sorry to those people," said Natalie.

Stacey looked at me but I quickly looked down at my shoes because how could I tell her what happened? This was getting worse and worse.

"What are you talking about?" asked Stacey.

"Didn't she tell you what she did?" asked Melissa.

"Didn't who tell me what *who* did?"

"Why, Rose, of course. Didn't she tell you how mean she was to Hailey and Bailey and that she told the teacher lies about them and got them into trouble?"

"You know that's not true!" I said.

"Well, that's what Hailey said happened," said Melissa.

"Yes, Hailey and Bailey told all the kids everything you did," said Paige.

I felt like my nose wasn't working anymore and I couldn't even breath air in.

"But you know that's not true!" I said again.

Natalie was looking at me and I looked right into her face and I said, "Natalie, you've known me already for such a long time. You know I'm not some mean person like that."

Natalie still didn't say anything and she wasn't even looking at me.

"YOU KNOW IT'S NOT TRUE!!" I shouted.

I couldn't even look at them. I could feel the tears starting in my eyes and I couldn't even look at Stacey. I knew she was looking at me. I knew Paige and Melissa were all looking at me. I could feel them looking at me. When I blinked my eyes, the tears just started to roll down on my cheeks. I didn't know what to do. I felt like I couldn't do anything anymore. Well, maybe just one thing. I could still do one thing. I could run.

I ran and I ran until I was all the way on the other side of the yard and I ran under the slide where I knew they wouldn't see me. I sat there on the ground under the slide and I really started crying. The kind of crying when you don't even know that you're making sounds, but you hear there are crying noises coming from you. The kind of crying that comes not from your eyes but from deep, deep in your chest.

I heard the school bell ring telling everyone recess was over, but I didn't care. I heard everyone running to line up at the doors, but I didn't care about that either. Once I started crying I just couldn't stop it and there was just no way to fix this. Mom tried and Mrs. Sharpe tried and I tried and it was just getting worse and worse.

Now I bet you that even Stacey hates me. She thinks I'm this terrible, mean person, who makes up lies about other people just to get them into trouble. I can't tell her what happened because then I'll hurt her feelings if I tell her that Hailey and Bailey didn't want her at my party. And even if I did tell her the truth, she probably won't believe me now, because everyone thinks I'm this terrible, mean person.

I'm never going to come out from under the slide. I'll wait until it gets really dark, when everyone goes home and then I'll run away and then

everyone will miss me. Maybe if I just lie down here on the ground it'll be easier to wait until it gets dark.

I can see the last person go into the school now from recess and the doors close. Good, now all I have to do is wait here for two more recesses and then I can go.

"Rose, where are you?" shouted Mrs. Sharpe. "Recess is over. You have to come inside now, Rose."

Mrs. Sharpe is walking around the schoolyard looking for me. She's walking fast and calling me over and over. I think she's really worried. I didn't mean to make her worry. I like Mrs. Sharpe and it's not her fault this happened. Well, it's kind of her fault because she told me a sleepover party was a good idea. Boy, was she wrong. And then she told me I could fix this if we spoke together to Hailey and Bailey. Boy, was she wrong. Now that I think about it, she *should* be worried about me. I'm glad she's worried.

"Rose!" shouted Mrs. Sharpe. "This isn't like you. You have to come in right now. Recess is over!"

I could see Mrs. Sharpe getting closer to the slide. Suddenly she bent down and looked right at me.

"Rose," Mrs. Sharpe asked, "what are you doing under there?"

I didn't want to talk to her.

"Does this have something to do with what happened before in the classroom? Is this still the problem you're having with Hailey and Bailey?"

I still couldn't say anything so I just nodded my head up and down to mean yes.

"I think we need to go into the class and solve this," said Mrs. Sharpe. "I think that if we explain to Hailey and Bailey that you misunderstood and then you apologize to them, well, they're nice girls, I'm sure they'll forgive you and this will all be over."

When I heard that Mrs. Sharpe wanted me

to say I was sorry to Hailey and Bailey I couldn't even believe that idea. I finally managed to say just one thing to Mrs. Sharpe.

"Call my mother. I want to go home, please, please Mrs. Sharpe. I don't feel good. I think I'm really sick. Yes, I feel really sick and I have to go home."

7

Stacey and Me

Mrs. Sharpe made me go with her to the office while they called my mom on the phone. They told her that I wasn't feeling well and that I wanted to go home. As soon as my mom walked into the office, I started crying again.

"Rose, sweetheart, what's wrong?" mom asked.

"I feel sick," I said.

"Where does it feel sick?"

"Everywhere," I said.

Mom sat next to me and looked me right in

my eyes for a minute. She didn't say anything. She put her arms around me and gave me a big hug.

"I think we should go home," she said, and then she got up to sign the book in the office that tells that you're going home.

I didn't say anything the whole drive home. I felt a little better sitting with my mom in the car and I stopped crying, but I still had this sick feeling all over me. When we got home, mom held my hand and we went into the kitchen.

"Rose, do you feel like telling me what happened at school after I left?" she asked.

"Oh, Mom, it was just terrible. It was the worst day I can ever remember in my life," I said.

"Do you want to tell me about it?"

And then I told her everything. I told her about Hailey and Bailey and how all the girls won't talk to me now. I told her that now even Stacey thinks I'm this mean, terrible person. I told her that everyone thinks I should say I'm sorry to Hailey and Bailey.

"Do you think I should say I'm sorry?" I asked.

"No, I don't," mom said. "I think that you've had a very hard day today and maybe we need a nice break. Why don't we sit together and watch one of your favorite shows and we can talk about all this later. How does that sound?"

"Boy, what a great idea. I don't think I can think about this anymore, it's already hurting my brain. Can we watch cartoons?" I asked.

"Sure," said mom. "You go find cartoons on the television and I'll be there right after I make us a great snack."

So I spent the rest of the day sitting in front of the TV with my mom close to me, eating the fruit she brought for us. After that, she popped popcorn for us to share.

Just as we were starting to eat the popcorn, the doorbell rang and mom went to see who it was.

"Rose," called mom, "Stacey's at the door."

I didn't know what to do. What if she's really mad at me, or what if she came over to tell me she doesn't want to be my friend anymore because I'm this terrible, mean person? Suddenly my stomach started hurting.

"Hi, Rose," Stacey said when she came in the room.

"Hi, Stacey," I said.

"Are you okay? My mom brought me over after school because I told her you went home sick. She's talking to your mom in the kitchen. Are you feeling better?" she asked.

"I don't know yet," I said. "My mom is sitting with me until we figure it out."

Stacey and I sat together and ate the popcorn and watched the cartoons.

"I love this cartoon, don't you?" Stacey asked.

"Yeah, it's one of my favorites," I said.

"Mine too," Stacey said.

We ate some more popcorn.

"I think this is the funniest cartoon of my life, don't you?" Stacey asked.

"Yeah, I do too," I said.

The popcorn was almost finished and the only things left in the bowl were the unpopped kernels at the bottom.

"I hate the kernels, don't you?" asked Stacey.

"Yeah, they get stuck in my teeth," I said.

"Mine too," said Stacey.

I started to feel a little bit better. This was the same old Stacey. My friend. Why did I think she would believe those girls today? I really love Stacey.

"Do you want to see my new deck of cards?" I asked.

"Sure, yeah, that sounds great," Stacey said.

I went to the cupboard and took out my cards.

"I love these pictures on your cards," said Stacey. "They show 3-D when you move them in the light. I love that, don't you?"

"Yeah, they're my favorite kind," I said.

"Mine too," said Stacey.

We sat and played 'Spit' together and then Stacey said, "I have a new game we can play with your cards."

"What kind of game?" I asked.

"Well, it goes like this. First we divide up the cards into two piles and then we each get a piece of paper. Then each of us has to flip one card from her pile. The person with the highest card gets to write a letter from her name. Then the first person to finish writing yells 'Bingo' and the other person has to put her cards down and then we add up how much is left in the card piles and the person with the most cards left wins the game."

"Okay, that sounds like fun," I said, though I don't remember playing a game where you win when you have more cards than the other person, but Stacey always has strange game rules and they end up fun anyway.

I got the paper and we started our writing race. Soon I was laughing and rolling on the floor with Stacey, just like always.

"I like this game, don't you?" asked Stacey.

"Yeah, I like it a lot," I said.

"Wanna hear something funny?" asked Stacey.

"Sure," I said.

"I remembered this joke after we played the spelling game today in school. I wanted to tell you but you'd already gone home. It's pretty funny. Are you ready?"

"Yeah, I'm ready," I said.

"What's the happiest day for a cow?" asked Stacey.

"I don't know," I said.

"Moo-ving day," she said.

Suddenly I started laughing and laughing.

"What's all the laughing in here?" my mom asked as she came into the room with Stacey's mom.

"Wanna hear something funny?" I asked.

"Sure," mom said.

"Why does a cow like moo-ving day?" I asked.

"That's not how it goes!" yelled Stacey. We both burst out laughing and couldn't stop.

"I don't know about this," mom said. "I guess it was funny before."

Stacey's mom started to giggle.

"These girls are laughing so hard, they're making me laugh," she said.

Before we knew what was happening, Stacey, her mom, my mom and me were all laughing so hard our bellies started to hurt and we finally had to stop and rest.

"Boy, that felt good," I said.

"Yes," said my mom, "I think we all needed that laugh after what happened today."

The room was suddenly very quiet. All the laughing stopped and I remembered my terrible day.

"Rose," said Stacey, "please tell me what happened today."

8

You're Not the Boss of Me

"Listen, Rose," Stacey said, "I didn't believe those girls today. I don't think that you would get someone into trouble just to be mean."

"I really wouldn't, you know," I said.

"Yeah, I know," she said. "What did happen?"

And this is when I had to make up my mind. If I tell Stacey what Hailey and Bailey said then I'll hurt her feelings. But maybe she knows why they're being so mean and maybe she can help fix this problem.

"Stacey, did you do something to Hailey or to Bailey?" I asked.

"What do you mean?" she asked.

"Did you guys have a fight or something? Did you say something to them or do something that got them mad?" I asked.

"No, nothing I can think of," she said. "What does that have to do with anything?"

Just then my mom interrupted us.

"Girls," said mom, "we want to talk to both of you about today. I've already talked to Stacey's mom and told her what went on at school."

"Can I know?" asked Stacey. "It seems everybody knows but me."

Now Stacey's mom sat next to her and told her what Hailey and Bailey said and how I tried to solve the problem. My mom explained to Stacey about our talk with Mrs. Sharpe and how Hailey and Bailey said they never did any of these things.

At first, Stacey was angry. "They didn't want

me to come to the party?" she asked. "Why would they say that?!"

Then Stacey got sad and cried a little bit.

"Why would they be so mean?" she asked.

Then Stacey wanted to know what I've been wondering about since all this started.

"What did I do to them?" she asked.

"Stacey, you didn't do anything," her mom said.

"That's the whole problem here," mom said. "Sometimes people are mean to each other and even though we try and try to understand it, there just isn't a good reason."

"Some people need to feel they have control over other people. They want to tell people what to do and how to do it for no good reason except they just want people to listen to them," Stacey's mom explained.

"Oh," I added, "they want to be the boss of you."

Mom smiled. "Yes, that's right. They want

74

to be the boss of you, so they'll tell you what you can and can't do. They may also say bad things about you or get other people to think bad things about you."

"That's what happened today," I said. "It was terrible."

"It's always terrible, and it always hurts," mom said.

"What are we supposed to do?" asked Stacey.

"Here's the hard part, girls, so you need to listen carefully," my mom began. "You can't stop other people from saying things. Sometimes people try to do that, but usually it doesn't work. If you try to control them then you're doing the same thing they did."

"But there is something you can control," Stacey's mom added. "You are the only one who can give in and let them be the boss of you, or you can take their power away."

"It's easy to give in," my mom said. "Rose, if you had uninvited Stacey and told her not to come to your sleepover party, that would have been giving in. It would have hurt Stacey but then the problem would have gone away for a while. That's what makes it easy."

"I could never do that," I said.

"I know," mom said. "But, it's really hard not to give in. It's really hard to do what you know inside is the right thing. When you listen to yourself and do what you know is right, then you take their power away and eventually they stop noticing you. The very hard part is that this takes a really long time to happen. During that time these girls might think of even more mean things to do. They want to feel important so they'll keep trying until they decide it won't work with you."

"That's why this is so hard," said Stacey's mom. "It takes a very long time and it usually gets worse before it gets better. That's why most people give in, just to make the problem go away."

"We think you girls can be strong enough not to give in," said my mom.

"You two girls are such good friends, you can share this together," said Stacey's mom.

"That's important," mom said. "When you go back to school tomorrow the other girls might not play with you or talk to you. They may say things that hurt. I know how much you're going to want to run away from it, Rose. I understand what happened today. But tomorrow, remember that you two have each other and you can help each other get through this."

"If Hailey and Bailey see you get mad tomorrow, then they'll think they're the boss of you because they can get you so mad," explained Stacey's mom.

"If Hailey and Bailey see you are both sad tomorrow, it's the same thing," added my mom.

"So how are we supposed to behave?" I asked.

"Just be normal," mom said.

"Just be yourselves," Stacey's mom said.

"Let them know that they are not the boss of

you and that they don't even make you mad or sad," mom said.

"That's why this is so hard," Stacey's mom said. "You both have to be very strong."

"I don't know," Stacey said. "I don't know if I can do this. Do we have to go back to school tomorrow?"

"Girls," said Stacey's mom, "it's important that this doesn't stop you from going to school or doing the things you want to do."

"The best way to stop this kind of thing is to not give control to these kids," my mom said. "Do you understand what we're saying?"

"Mom," I said, "I think I understand. I know this is going to be really hard. I know that if no one else plays with us then Stacey and I can play together and that'll be okay. I know that the mean things they say will make me mad, but I'll try not to cry or let them be the boss of me. When I come home, I'll tell you how it feels and then it's okay to cry, right?"

Mom smiled. "Yes, Rose, it's always okay to let your feelings out at home and I can help you get strong for the next day."

"There's only one thing I'm still not sure about," I said.

"Yes, what is it?" asked mom.

"I get everything you said, but ... " Now I could feel the tears starting to come back into my eyes.

"What is it, Rose?" asked mom.

"What if nobody comes to my party?"

9

Conversations

That night I didn't sleep very well. I kept rolling in my bed and just couldn't get comfortable. Soon my pillow felt too hot, and I had to turn it over to get the cool side. Then my blankets felt too heavy, and I kicked them off. Then I felt too cold, and I pulled them back on.

After a while I knew I just wasn't going to fall asleep so I decided to turn on my lamp and read some of my favorite books. Even though I like chapter books a lot, I still also like picture books, but I don't tell too many people that. Sometimes kids think picture books are for babies and I don't want them to think I'm a baby. That's why I keep my picture books in my room where I can still read them but keep them private.

I love the picture books where there are animals. I mean, chapter books are okay, but in a picture book I can look at the picture and see all kinds of things that the words don't say. I like when all the animals become friends and solve a problem together. In the real world these animals don't all mix together. My picture books aren't about what happens in the real world.

I made a pile of six picture books and put them on my bed. I don't know exactly when I fell asleep, but in the morning the picture books were still on my bed.

"Good morning, sleepy cinnamon bun," said mom.

"Good morning, Mom," I said, yawning and stretching.

"Know why I call you a cinnamon bun in the morning?" my mom asked.

Of course I know. Mom asks me this almost every morning when she wakes me up.

"Because you love warm cinnamon buns and I smell warm and sweet in the morning," I said, rolling my eyes. Mom thinks I'm still a baby.

"That's right," said mom. "Know what else I like in the morning?"

This was new. Mom never asked me about anything else she likes in the morning. I sat up in my bed and looked at her.

"I don't know," I said. "What else do you like in the morning?"

"Hot, mushy oatmeal," she said.

I stared at her, not sure why she was telling me this. After thinking about it for just one minute I realized why she was telling me about the hot mushy oatmeal.

"Oh, no, please Mom, please don't … "

"Good morning, my hot mushy oatmeal," she said with a big smile.

"Oh, no," I groaned. All I need is another morning nickname but I guess mom is just trying to cheer me up so I'll pretend it's working.

"Better get up and washed and dressed," mom said.

"Are you going to call me that every morning now?" I asked.

"Of course not," she said, "that's way too long a name."

"Oh, thank goodness," I said.

"I'll just call you 'hot mush' for short," mom said.

My mouth dropped open when she said that. But then I suddenly started laughing because that was just one of the funniest things I've heard in my life.

"See, there's always a way to start the day with a smile," said mom.

I got up, I got washed, I got dressed, I ate my

breakfast, and I even started putting on my shoes before I remembered about school and started to get that feeling in my stomach again.

"Mom, I'm scared," I said as we were driving to school.

"I know you are," she said. "Just keep remembering the things we talked about yesterday. Remember what a good friend Stacey is and that in a few hours we'll sit together and talk about your day."

"What if I start to feel sick again?" I asked.

"You might feel that way again today," mom said. "If you do, ask to go to the washroom and splash some water on your face. Sometimes I find that getting a minute by myself can help me when I feel that way."

"Okay, I'll try," I said. "I'm still scared though."

"I know, sweetheart. I wish I could go with you today, but you know that wouldn't fix this."

"Yeah, I know," I said.

I gave mom a huge, tight, squeezy hug, and then I got out of the car. I ran into the schoolyard and got on one of the swings. I decided I was just going to wait for Stacey to come and not even try to talk to anyone.

"Hi, Rose," said Kirstin.

"Oh, hi, Kirstin," I said.

"Are you feeling better?" she asked.

"Yeah, kind of," I said.

"Good, sorry you got so sick yesterday," she said.

Just as I was thinking that maybe it wouldn't be so terrible today, Paige ran into the playground and Kirstin quickly left the swings and ran over to Paige. Kirstin didn't talk to me again all day.

Stacey and I spent the whole day together. We ate lunch together and we played all her new games.

"You know some of the girls are staring at us," Stacey said.

"Yeah, I know," I said.

"What do you think they're thinking?" she asked.

"I don't know," I said. "Why, do you want to ask them?"

Stacey gasped. "Are you kidding?"

"Yeah," I smiled. "Of course I'm kidding."

In class, Mrs. Sharpe gave us books to read and spelling games and we had math centers. It was a busy day, which was really good because nobody had any time to say anything or talk about what was going on.

At the afternoon recess, Stacey and I played all her new games, though we had to change some of the rules because it was just the two of us. When school was over, mom picked me up and we were walking to our car when Jessica's mom stopped to talk.

"I hear there's a problem with the sleepover party," Jessica's mom said.

"What do you mean?" my mom asked her.

"I'm not even quite sure what it's all about,

but I feel strongly that Jessica makes her own decisions about her friends," she said.

"Well, Jessica is always welcome to come to the party," mom said. "We'll be more than happy if she decides to come."

Just then, Hailey's mom walked over toward our car and butted right into the conversation.

"Is this about Rose's party?" she asked. "I heard what went on, but I decided not to intervene. I mean, really, my Hailey isn't having any problems, so I don't think I should get involved."

Hailey's mom talks with her hands a lot. I noticed that her nail polish matched her lipstick and her lipstick was exactly the same color as the lipstick Hailey brings at recess. I watched her hands moving all around and then I waited to hear what my mom would say.

Mom watched Hailey's mom for a minute and then said, "I believe that if we don't get involved in these things then we send our kids the wrong message. It might seem that it's a small problem now, but it easily grows out of control. You may think that Hailey is not part of this problem, but anyone who knows about it is part of it."

"As I said, I leave all these decisions for my daughter to make," Jessica's mom said. "I think we adults should just stay out of it. How will they learn to think for themselves?"

"I don't agree with you," my mom said with a sigh. "Sometimes our kids need a bit of help figuring these things out. Again, we'll be happy to have Jessica and Hailey join us."

We walked to our car and got in.

"Do you think they're going to come to the party?" I asked.

"You know what honey," said mom, "I just don't know."

That night when I got home, mom and I sat and talked about the day. It wasn't a great day, but it wasn't the most terrible day either.

"You'll see," mom said, "tomorrow might not

be much better, but in a few days it should start getting a little better."

"Yeah, well, maybe," I said. Mom hadn't said anything about my party and it was only one week away.

"Are we still going to go shopping for my party?" I asked.

"Of course we are," she answered. "How are we going to have the best party ever if we don't get all our supplies?"

"How do we know how many people are coming?" I asked.

"Well, let's assume that everyone who said they're going to come is still going to come," mom said. "Who said they couldn't make it?"

"Um, only Hailey and Bailey said they wouldn't come," I said, "but all the girls are playing with them at recess and no one is talking to me and Stacey so I don't know if the other girls are going to come."

"The best thing to do, remember, is to go

about things normally. If Hailey and Bailey said they can't come, then that means two girls will be missing. We'll buy all our supplies for everyone else you invited and assume that if they said they're coming, then they're still coming."

"Do you really think all those girls are going to come?" I asked. For the first time I started to feel like maybe this party could still be kind of a good one.

"No, sweetheart, I don't think they're all going to come. I think it's important for us to plan just as we were going to plan before, but we shouldn't get our hopes up about everybody coming. I'm not sure how many girls will show up. But there is one thing I am sure of," my mom said.

"What's that?" I asked.

"I'm sure that you will be there. I'm sure that Stacey will be there. I'm sure that I will be there. I'm sure that Stacey's mom will be there. I'm sure that all of us are going to build the weirdest, strangest, craziest pizzas you ever saw in your life.

I'm sure that we'll do wild hairdos and tell scary and probably horribly gross stories. What was that about mice hanging by their tails over the bathroom sink?" Mom rolled her eyes, stuck out her tongue and made a gross, gagging sound.

Okay, I thought, maybe not the worst party in the history of parties.

10

The Troublesome Note

Tuesday was my real birthday. My family had a birthday dinner with my parents and my grandparents and some of my cousins and aunts and uncles. There was a cake and they sang Happy Birthday. It was nice but it wasn't my real party. My real party was in a few days.

"Are you getting excited about Saturday night?" asked Stacey.

"I'm so scared. I don't know what's going to happen," I said.

"Who's coming?" Stacey asked.

"Stacey, you know I don't know that," I said. "You know that it could be that nobody is going to come. You know that my stomach feels like somebody is knitting a sweater in there because I'm so scared that nobody is going to come. Why do you ask me who's coming when you know I don't know?!" I was almost shouting.

"Wow," said Stacey. "I was just wondering if anybody called your house or said anything to your mom. I didn't know you were that scared. I'm sorry," she said.

Now I felt bad. "I'm sorry too," I said. "I mean I'm supposed to go shopping with my mom today after school and the party is tomorrow night and for all I know nobody is going to show up."

"I'll be there," said Stacey.

I gave Stacey a big hug. I knew that this wasn't so much fun for her either all week with nobody still talking to us. I guess she felt as bad as I did.

"You know what?" I asked.

"What?" asked Stacey.

"Let's promise right now to have fun no matter what happens."

"Yeah," said Stacey, "let's promise."

"Let's pinky-swear it," I said.

"Yeah," said Stacey, "let's pinky-swear it."

We both put out our pinky fingers and linked them together and then as we swung our hands back and forth we made our pinky-swear together. Having fun no matter what happens, boy, that was going to be a hard pinky-swear to keep.

On Friday, right after school, mom and I went shopping for all our supplies for the party. Here is the list of things we bought:

pizza dough
pizza sauce
green peppers
mushrooms
red peppers

green olives with red pimientos inside
yellow cheese all shredded up
orange cheese all shredded up
white cheese all shredded up

And then of course we got all the fun supplies.
Here is the list of the fun stuff we bought:

red nail polish
pink nail polish
cotton balls
flashlights
extra batteries
loot bags
stickers for the loot bags
plastic rings and bracelets for the
loot bags
plastic puzzles and magic tricks for the
loot bags

And of course …

BIRTHDAY CAKE!

The bakery wrote my name in purple icing on the white vanilla frosting that covered my big fat chocolate cake. I don't like flowers on my cake so we asked them to please put little plastic figures on it, which I like better than the sugar flowers for decorations.

When we got home, mom and I put together all the loot bags and put everything into the fridge so it would be fresh for tomorrow. I counted nine loot bags. I went over the list in my head. Here's who was supposed to be coming:

Stacey
Paige
Melissa
Judy
Kirstin

Kim
Ashley
Natalie
Kaitlin

Of course, who could forget who wasn't coming …

Hailey and Bailey.

"We need to set up the basement for the sleeping bags," my mom said.

"I know," I said. "I'll get paper and markers from my backpack so that I can sketch out who sleeps next to who."

When I opened my backpack, I saw my paper and markers right where I had put them, but folded up in the front was a note with my name printed in red marker.

The note said,

Dear Rose,

I really really wish I could come to your party. It sounds like it will really be so much fun. But I can't come because Hailey knows a secret about me. One day I made a big mistake and I told her that I really liked someone in the class. I even told her the name of the person I liked! Can you believe it? Every day I worry all day that Hailey is going to tell. Well today she told me that if I go to your party, she'll tell everyone my secret. So as much as I would love to come, I can't.

I just wanted to tell you I'm sorry.

Signed,
Your friend.

"Mom, Mom!" I shouted. "Look at this!"

Mom came quickly into the room and I showed her the note. She read it over a couple of times.

"Rose, you notice that your friend didn't sign

her name," my mom said. "It looks like Hailey has her so scared that she can't even say who she is."

"But we have to help her, don't we?" I asked.

"How are we going to help her if we don't know who she is?" mom answered. "You can't solve everybody's problems. I understand that's hard and it doesn't feel right."

"It really doesn't feel right. I feel terrible for her," I said.

"I agree and we should feel terrible, but if you don't know who it is, it's impossible to help her," mom said.

"But she sounds so sad," I said. "And she really, really wants to come to my party."

"Well, honey," mom said. "Maybe she'll tell an adult what's going on and they'll help her make the right decision."

"You mean, maybe she'll still come to my party?" I asked.

"Maybe," mom said. "Let's hope she talks to either her mom or dad."

"How do kids know when to ask their parents for help?" I asked. "'Cause Mrs. Sharpe says we should try to solve problems by ourselves before we go to grown-ups. And grown-ups always know when to ask for help and when not to so I can't figure this out."

"Well," mom said, "like right now I'm going to ask you to help me set up the basement for your party."

So we spent the next hour clearing away space in the basement for the sleeping bags. We also brought down some extra sheets, blankets, and pillows. Mom even thought to bring in a night-light, just in case any of my friends couldn't sleep without one.

"If we need anything else, should we ask you?" I asked my mom.

"Yes," she said.

"So, we should always ask a grown-up for help, right?" I asked.

"No," mom answered.

"Well, then, I don't get it." I was worried. "You said my friend should ask her parents for help and then you said I should ask you for help if any of my friends need anything, so how do I know when I ask for help and when I solve it myself?"

"Rose," mom said, "that's a really important question. Whenever you're not sure what to do, you can always come and ask me what I think. With any problem, you should ask yourself if you know how to try and solve it. If you do, then you should try, but if you feel you just can't figure it out or it's just not working, then you should come and speak to me so we can solve it together."

"Like, right now, I don't know if I should put the pillow at the top of the sleeping bag or the bottom of the sleeping bag," I said with a giggle. "Can you solve that problem for me?"

"Sure," mom answered, "you should put all the pillows outside on the porch."

I looked at her for a minute because she sounded so serious about it, I just had to check.

I saw her smiling quietly and I knew she got my joke.

"You're so funny sometimes," mom said.

"Yeah," I said as I laid out the last cushion and blanket.

"Well," she said, "I think we're ready."

"Yup," I said.

I started to picture what things would look like tomorrow night. I already had my sleeping bag down on the floor in the basement so I knew where I would be sleeping. I knew that right next to me would be Stacey's sleeping bag. I just didn't know if anyone else would be showing up. I couldn't help but wonder how many other of my friends would really want to come to my party, but were just too afraid.

Will there be any other sleeping bags on the floor tomorrow night?

11

Arrivals

Finally, after what felt like so long I couldn't count the time anymore, finally, it was *finally* time for my birthday sleepover party.

"Shouldn't the doorbell be ringing yet?" I asked.

"Not yet," mom said. "It's still fifteen minutes until the time you put on your invitation. Why don't you check the table again to make sure we're ready?"

I don't know why mom keeps asking me to

check the table. Every time I ask her if it's time for my party, she tells me to check the table. I don't get it. How many times can I check the table? I think I've checked it at least twelve times.

"Mom," I shouted, "the table looks fine."

Just then the doorbell rang.

"I'LL GET IT!!!" I shouted as I zipped past my mom heading straight for the door.

"HI STACEY, ARE YOU READY FOR MY PARTY?" I shouted.

"Rose," my mom said, "you don't have to shout through the door, sweetheart. Just open the door and let your guests in. You can welcome them once they're in the house."

"Okay, Mom," I said. "Sorry."

I opened the door and let Stacey in. We ran downstairs to put her sleeping bag next to mine and I showed her where we set up for the pizza-making and where we set up for the nail polish and where we set up for the hair party.

"Wow," Stacey said, "I'm so excited. I couldn't

wait all day long. I kept asking my mom if it was time to come yet and she kept telling me she'd let me know when it was time to come."

"Yeah," I said, "I was pretty excited too, but I don't think I was bothering my mom, I think I hid it really well."

"Rose, there's someone at the door," mom called down the stairs.

I zipped past my mom, heading straight for the door.

"HI JUDY!" I shouted through the door. "ARE YOU READY FOR MY PARTY?"

"Rose, honey," mom said, "just open the door and greet your guest inside the house, please."

"Oh, sorry Mom," I said.

I opened the door and let Judy into the house. Her mom was standing with her and she said hi to my mom.

"What a great idea to have a sleepover party," said Judy's mom. "I know there was some silliness going on with some of the girls at school. Never you mind that silliness. Judy was really excited about coming."

"Thank you," mom said. "We're glad to have her."

"See you tomorrow," said Judy's mom as she walked back to her car.

"Bye, Mom!" shouted Judy.

"Come on downstairs," I said, "I'll show you where to put your sleeping bag. Stacey's already here."

"Okay," said Judy. "My mom couldn't wait to bring me. She kept asking me to look on the invitation and see if it was time to come yet."

"Well," I said, "I'm glad you're here. We're going to have so much fun."

I showed Judy where to put her sleeping bag and where we're going to make pizza and where we're going to do our nails and before I could show her our hair stuff, I heard my mom.

"Rose," called mom, "you have a guest at the door."

I zipped past my mom, heading straight for the door.

"HI NATALIE!" I shouted through the door. "ARE YOU READY FOR MY PARTY?"

Mom opened the door and told Natalie we were really happy she could come. Natalie's mom unstrapped the sleeping bag and backpack from the back of her bike and passed them to Natalie.

"There's no way Natalie was going to miss this party," her mom said. "I was telling Natalie that when I was her age I remember there was this one girl in my class who tried to take control of everything. I wasn't going to let Natalie fall into that trap."

I showed Natalie where to put her sleeping bag and then Stacey and Judy right away showed Natalie where the pizza stuff was and the nail stuff and the hair stuff.

Just as I finished getting Natalie downstairs into the basement, I heard mom shouting.

"Rose, you have ... "

Once again, I zipped past my mom, heading straight for the door.

"HI KIRSTIN! ARE YOU READY FOR MY PARTY?"

I quickly ran downstairs to show Kirstin where all the girls were putting down their sleeping bags.

And then the doorbell didn't ring any more.

12

My Sleepover Party

My sleepover party was smaller than I ever thought a sleepover party could be. From eleven invitations that I gave out at school, only Stacey, Judy, Natalie, and Kirstin showed up. Only four girls came to a party where eleven girls were supposed to come.

The party was smaller than I imagined it. Instead of eleven pizzas we made five pizzas, including mine. Mom, dad and Stacey's mom also made pizzas. But theirs don't really count 'cause they were grown up pizzas. I was feeling kind of sad because there were only four girls at my sleepover party.

"Mom?" I asked in the kitchen when we were alone for a minute, "do you think anyone else is going to come to my party?"

"No, sweetheart, I don't think so," mom answered.

I looked at my pizza with its red pepper mouth and green olive eyes and green pepper hair and mushroom nose.

"Are you feeling okay that only four friends came?" my mom asked.

"Well," I said, "it's too bad that the party's so small, don't you think?"

"Well," mom said. "I think the girls who did come are very special friends."

"Why?" I asked.

"They came to your party even though most other girls didn't. These girls knew that what Hailey and Bailey did was wrong and ... "

"They wouldn't let them be the bosses of them," I said.

"That's right," mom said.

I thought about that for a minute. Then I ran downstairs to my friends and turned on my flashlight and told them the scariest, grossest, funniest story I ever heard.

"And then she hung the mice by their tails over the sink," I said.

"OOOOOOOOHHHH!" shouted the girls.

"That's gross!" shouted Stacey.

"That's gross plus one!" shouted Judy.

"That's gross plus infinity!" shouted Natalie.

"That's gross plus infinity and one!" shouted Kirstin.

"Pizzas are ready!" shouted mom.

The rest of the night we ate, did our nails, made crazy hairdos, and told spooky stories. I don't remember when I fell asleep, but I remember that I woke up with my friends and my mom and dad made delicious pancakes for everyone.

We all ate and told 'remember when' stories about last night, which I love the best of any sleepover.

"Remember when you turned in your sleep and stuck your thumb in my nose?" I said to Stacey.

"I did not!" Stacey shouted back, laughing. "But I remember when you started snoring and you were so loud the dog next door started barking to try and drown you out."

"That's nothing," said Natalie. "Remember when we were doing your nails and you tried to draw a happy face on my big toe?"

"I did not," said Kirstin. "But it came out really nice, didn't it?"

We kept doing 'remember whens' and laughing and eating and didn't even notice all the time was gone until Judy's mom rang the doorbell to pick her up.

"I had a great time," said Judy.

"My mom just drove up too," said Kirstin.

Before I knew it, everyone had been picked up and was gone and only me and Stacey were left in the kitchen.

"I had the best time," said Stacey. "Thank you for inviting me to your party."

"There's no way I could have a party if you weren't there," I said.

Stacey's mom knocked on the door and we ran to get her stuff. The whole rest of the day I helped mom clean up and before you knew it, you couldn't even see that there ever was a party in my basement.

I lay in bed that night feeling good about the party, but feeling really scared about going to school tomorrow. What will Hailey and Bailey do? What will they say? Will all the girls still ignore me? Do they all think I'm still this terrible, mean person who tells lies about people just to get them into trouble and then doesn't even say she's sorry when the teacher tells her that the best thing to do would be to say you're sorry?

I didn't get much sleep that night.

13

Facing Tomorrow

The next morning I could barely pay any attention to Mrs. Sharpe the whole time she was explaining something new. I'm not even sure what she was explaining and now I'm not sure how I'm going to do the homework. All I could think was that recess was coming up.

When the bell rang, we all lined up and I looked up and down the line, just to make sure that Stacey was still there and going out to play. Once we got outside, I ran over to Stacey and she suggested playing her new game, 'throw the ball up and clap six times before spinning around and catching the ball.'

Suddenly I noticed that Paige was watching us playing this game. She wasn't coming over, she wasn't shouting hello or saying anything. She just stood by the swings and watched us. Paige didn't come to my party and I'm not really sure why not, but I smiled at her because Paige had always been my friend.

I looked close at her and noticed that she started to smile back at me. Stacey was still playing 'throw the ball, clap and spin' so I decided to go over and at least just say 'Hi' to Paige and then come right back. But then a very strange thing happened. Just as I started to walk over to Paige, she suddenly stopped smiling. As soon as she knew I was walking over to her, she turned around and walked away from me towards Hailey and Bailey who were playing with the other girls in our class.

I felt a warm, hot and hurting feeling inside me. I didn't want it spreading to my eyes, so I took a deep breath and counted to three before letting my breath go. Then I turned back to Stacey for my turn.

14

Looking Back

I know what happened to me is a very long story and sometimes I still feel sad when I think about the whole thing. Hailey and Bailey are in another classroom now so I don't think about them too much, but I'll never forget what happened.

I'm glad I could tell you all about it. I know it happened to me last year and maybe you think that's so long ago that really, why would I tell you this whole, long, story?

Well, I just heard that you're having a party

and you're not sure who to invite. One thing I learned is you make your decisions on your own without anyone else being the boss and telling you who to be friends with.

Your worst sleepover party is the one where you leave out good kids for no good reason. Your best sleepover party is when you know you did what your inside told you was right, even if it doesn't end up being the party you imagined.

My worst sleepover party really turned into my best because that was the birthday party where I only turned one year older but I felt like I really grew up.

❀

Resources

For more perspectives on the problem of bullying, please see the following resources:

Recommended Fiction
Agnes Parker Girl in Progress by Kathleen O'Dell, (Penguin, 2004)
Blubber by Judy Blume, (Yearling, 1986)
Just Kidding by Trudy Ludwig; Illustrated by Adam Gustavson, (Tricycle Press, 2006)
My Secret Bully by Trudy Ludwig & Abigail Marble; Illustrated by Susan Wellman, (Tricycle Press, 2005)
Secret Friends by Elizabeth Laird, (Hodder & Stoughton, 2000)
The Girls by Amy Koss, (Penguin USA, 2002)

Websites
Bullying in Schools and what to do –
http://www.education.unisa.edu.au/bullying/
Bully Beware – **http://www.bullybeware.com/**
Bully reporting site, with "toolbox" –
http://www.bullystoppers.com/
http://clubophelia.com/
http://www.stoptextbully.org/
http://www.cyberbully.org/
http://www.cyberbullying.org/
http://www.kidshealth.org/kid/feeling/
http://www.bullying.org
http://www.kidshelpphone.ca/en/
http://www.talk-helps.com/

For a complete list, please see **http://www.secondstorypress.ca**.